mary-kateandashley

It's a Twin Thing

Look for these

titles:

mary-kateandashley

TWO of a kind ™

It's a Twin Thing

Adapted by Judy Katschke

from the teleplay by Howard Adler and Bob Griffard

from the series created by Robert Griffard
& Howard Adler

TED SMART

A PARACHUTE PRESS BOOK
Parachute Publishing, L.L.C.
156 Fifth Avenue
Suite 325
NEW YORK
NY 10010

First published in the USA by Harper*Entertainment* 1999
First published in Great Britain by Collins 2002
HarperCollins*Entertainment* is an imprint of HarperCollins*Publishers* Ltd,
77-85 Fulham Palace Road, Hammersmith, London W6 8JB

Cover photo by George Lange

The HarperCollins website address is
www.**fire**and**water**.com

1 3 5 7 9 8 6 4 2

ISBN 0 00 766749 3

Printed and bound in Great Britain by Bookmarque Ltd, Croydon, Surrey

CHAPTER ONE

"Twenty hours to go," Mary-Kate Burke reported as she rode up the escalator at the mall. Checking her calendar watch, she wished it was fast – a whole month fast!

Her twin sister, Ashley, tapped her on the shoulder. "Did you say something, Mary-Kate?"

"Our hours of freedom are numbered," Mary-Kate declared. "Doesn't that mean anything to you?"

Ashley blew her blond fringe out of her eyes. "Mary-Kate, it's just the last day of summer vacation. Not the end of the world."

"Oh, yeah? Well, it is for me," Mary-Kate grumbled. "I am not looking forward to seventh grade! Especially with Miss Tandy. I hear she's the toughest teacher in the whole city of Chicago!"

She glanced over her shoulder at her father, Kevin Burke, who stood a few steps behind them on the escalator.

"Okay, girls," Kevin said as they reached the top. "We had our frozen yogurts and chicken fajitas. Now you have exactly one hour to find your back-to-school outfits."

"How about a prison uniform?" Mary-Kate muttered.

"Nah," Ashley said. She looked Mary-Kate up and down. "Orange isn't your colour."

"Ha, ha." Mary-Kate tugged at her oversize T-shirt. She hated going shopping. Unless it was for baseball caps, knee pads, sneakers . . .

"Here it is," Ashley gushed as they entered Bailey's department store. They walked into a section filled with skinny black jeans, colourful sweaters, and T-shirts. "My idea of paradise – the girls' department!"

Mary-Kate groaned when she saw all the signs that read BACK TO SCHOOL. Talk about in-your-face!

"Hey, girls," Kevin said. He held up a pink dress with big blue dots and a white collar. "How about this nifty number?"

Mary-Kate rolled her eyes. She might not be interested in fashion, but even she could tell that her dad's taste in clothes was . . . well, a little behind the times.

"Dad, please," Ashley whispered. She glanced around to make sure no one was looking. "We're eleven years old. We're going into the seventh grade. Not pre-school."

"Yeah," Mary-Kate agreed. "Think of our reputations."

Kevin shrugged as he hung the pink dress back on the rack. "Girls wore this when I was in seventh grade."

"They also had dinosaurs for pets," Mary-Kate shot back.

Kevin shook his head. "Impossible. The dinosaur became extinct ages before man first appeared— "

"Uh-oh." Ashley sighed. "Lecture number five thousand and fifty-three."

Mary-Kate grinned. "What else is new?" Having a college professor for a dad meant a lot of lectures. Lectures during breakfast, dinner, a drive – even while taking out the trash!

"Dad." Ashley interrupted their father, who was still talking about dinosaurs. She pointed to a row of chairs next to the elevators. "Why don't you have a

3

seat with the other bored dads while Mary-Kate and I try on clothes?"

"It's a deal," Kevin said. He pressed his palms together. "But please – only one outfit apiece. I'm still paying the credit card bill from the last time you two went shopping."

"Calm down, Dad," Mary-Kate said. "I just need a new pair of jeans. And maybe some new studs for my baseball sneakers."

"Speak for yourself," Ashley said. She waited until Kevin was out of the way. Then she grabbed Mary-Kate's arm.

"All systems go," she whispered. "We'll start with sportswear and work our way up to party clothes – just in case we're really popular this year!"

Sighing, Mary-Kate watched Ashley trot toward a table piled with sweaters. Her neat white shorts and cotton cardigan said it all – when it came to clothes, Ashley meant business!

"Which do you like better?" Ashley called as she held up two sweaters. "The grey or the red? I think the grey might bring out our blue eyes better – but this red looks great with blonde hair."

"I don't care. I'll take whichever one doesn't itch," Mary-Kate said, joining her sister at the sweater table.

Ashley rolled her eyes. "How can we be twins and have such totally different tastes?" she demanded.

"Well, we're not identical twins," Mary-Kate pointed out. "Even though most people have trouble telling us apart."

Ashley tossed the sweaters back on the table.

"Why am I the only one in this family who loves to shop?"

"Mom loved to shop," Mary-Kate said. "Remember?"

A slow, sad smile spread across Ashley's face. "Yeah. Mom used to say that if she had just one day to live, she'd spend it at the mall."

Mary-Kate chuckled, but deep inside she felt sad, too.

Their mom didn't spend her last day at the mall. She spent it in the hospital. The twins were just eight years old when she died – but Mary-Kate remembered every detail as if it happened only yesterday.

"Mom was so much fun," Mary-Kate said. "I really miss her."

"So do I," Ashley said. "Dad is great – but he's not a mom."

Mary-Kate nodded. Since their mom died, Kevin

had tried hard to be both mother and father to them. In fact, sometimes he tried too hard!

Ashley had gone back to picking sweaters. Mary-Kate stared. The pile in Ashley's arms almost reached her chin!

"Okay," Ashley called. "I'm all set. What are you going to try on, Mary-Kate?"

"I want an oversize jersey with a Cubs emblem on it," Mary-Kate decided.

"I don't see any of those around," Ashley said.

"That's because they're not in this section," Mary-Kate said. "They're in the boys' department. Let's go."

"The boys' department?" Ashley gasped. "You can't!"

"Why not?" Mary-Kate demanded. She hurried towards the other end of the floor. "Just because I'm a girl doesn't mean I have to dress like a total princess."

"Mary-Kate, wait!" Ashley called. "Don't go into the boys' dressing room... And I do not dress like a princess!"

Mary-Kate glanced over her shoulder and laughed. Ashley was trying to balance the tower of sweaters as she ran after her.

When Mary-Kate reached the boys' department, she spotted two boys from her school: Michael Cruz and a kid with light brown hair. He has some weird nickname, Mary-Kate thought. Something like Hokey . . . or Dopey . . . or . . .

Ashley ran up behind her, out of breath.

"Pokey," Mary-Kate remembered out loud. "Pokey Valentine."

Ashley gasped. "What?"

"That kid over there by the socks," Mary-Kate explained. "Pokey Valentine. He's in our class this year."

Ashley's head snapped to the side. She peered at Pokey. Then she ducked behind her pile of sweaters. Her cheeks turned red.

"Pokey Valentine? Oh, wow!" she whispered.

Mary-Kate stared at her sister. "What's with you? Why are you acting like such a weirdo?"

"I'm not!" Ashley protested.

"Whatever." Mary-Kate picked up a baseball cap. As she tried it on, she felt Ashley jab her in the shoulder with one finger.

"Are you sure Pokey Valentine is in our class this year?" Ashley asked quietly. "Who told you? How do you know?"

"I saw him at a baseball game this summer," Mary-Kate explained. "He said he has Miss Tandy – just like we do."

Ashley shoved the pile of sweaters into Mary-Kate's arms. Then she spun around and started hurrying towards the escalator. "Wait. *Now* where are you going?" Mary-Kate called.

"I just remembered some stuff I have to buy," Ashley said.

"What stuff?" Mary-Kate asked.

Ashley stopped and glanced over her shoulder. "You know – lipstick, eye shadow, blusher."

"You mean *make-up?*" Mary-Kate shrieked.

"Shh!" Ashley hissed. She darted a glance at Pokey Valentine. "Not so loud. He'll hear you!"

Then Mary-Kate got it.

"Oh, no," she groaned. She pulled the baseball cap down over her eyes. "Ashley's got a crush!"

She glanced back at Kevin. He was still sitting with the other dads in the girls' department, reading a magazine. *Probably something fascinating, like* Global Warming Quarterly, Mary-Kate thought.

"It's hard enough talking to him about clothes," Ashley said.

Mary-Kate grinned. Ashley knew exactly what she was thinking! That was the cool thing about being twins. Sometimes they could almost read each other's minds.

8

"Yeah. I can't *imagine* talking to him about boys," she said.

"Me neither," Ashley agreed. "We need Mom for that."

"Or at least some kind of girl," Mary-Kate added.

Ashley sneaked one last peek at Pokey Valentine. "He is *so* cute," she breathed. "I can't wait for school to start!"

Then she turned to tell her father they were going down the escalator again.

Mary-Kate sighed. "I can wait," she said to herself as she followed her sister. "I definitely can!"

CHAPTER TWO

RRR-RRRRING! RRR-RRRRING!

"Cool your jets," Mary-Kate muttered into her pillow. She reached out to give the alarm clock's snooze button a whack. But all she could feel was the top of her night table.

Where did that clock go? Mary-Kate wondered sleepily.

RRR-RRRRING! RRR-RRRRING!

Her face still in the pillow, Mary-Kate felt around on the night table. No clock.

Oh, well. At least the ringing had stopped. Mary-Kate was drifting back to dreamland when she heard her sister's voice.

"I moved the clock. You can't keep hitting the

snooze button, Mary-Kate," Ashley said. "You have to get up for school!"

Mary-Kate opened one eye. Ashley stood over her. She was not only out of bed, but already dressed in her new black skirt and silky red shirt.

"You'll be late if you don't get out of bed right now," Ashley warned.

"I'm not going," Mary-Kate mumbled. "I'm sick."

"Sick?" Ashley repeated. "But it's the first day."

"I know." Mary-Kate yanked the covers over her head. "That's why I'm sick."

Ashley gazed down at her sister and put her hands on her hips. "If you can't face the first day of school, how are you ever going to get through the next two hundred?"

"Two *hundred*?" Mary-Kate moaned through the covers. "Arrgh!"

Ashley turned away. Shaking her head, she began to make her bed.

She and Mary-Kate shared a bedroom – but it looked more like two rooms in one. Ashley's bed was decked with rose-printed sheets. Mary-Kate's sheets were splashed with baseball team logos. Ashley's side of the room was always neat and organised. Mary-Kate's side usually looked as if a cyclone had just blown through it.

How can we be twins? Ashley wondered for the thousandth time.

Bed made, she propped her favourite stuffed bear on her pillow. It was always the final touch.

"Now for the fun stuff." Ashley headed for her dresser. Her new make-up was still tucked away in a paper bag – but not for long!

"Blusher, lipstick, eye shadow, mascara," Ashley said as she pulled out compacts and cases. "Check, check, check, check."

She dusted on blusher. Then she outlined her lips with purple. She sucked in her cheeks as she studied her reflection.

Perfect!

Suddenly Mary-Kate's reflection appeared over her shoulder. Her mouth hung open. Her blue eyes were perfectly round.

"Lipstick?" Mary-Kate cried. "What are you doing, Ashley?"

"I'm getting ready for seventh grade," Ashley said calmly.

"You're getting ready for big trouble," Mary-Kate warned. "When dad sees you, he's going to flip!"

Ashley unscrewed the cap from the mascara.

"You saw me get the make-up at the mall yesterday," she pointed out. "I bought it with my own allowance money. So what's the problem?"

Mary-Kate waved her arms in the air. "I thought you'd ease into it. A dab of lipstick one day, a little mascara two years later – you know, give Dad a chance to get used to it."

Ashley carefully applied the mascara. "It's not going to bother Dad. He probably won't even notice."

"Get real!" Mary-Kate cried. "He wouldn't let you wear make-up to last year's Hallowe'en party. And you were going as a clown!"

"That's because I was only ten," Ashley explained. "Now we're eleven – practically teenagers. Besides, if Mom were alive, she'd let me wear make-up. She'd probably even show me how to put it on."

"I don't know about that," Mary-Kate murmured. "Anyway, we're talking about Dad, not Mom."

"Mary-Kate, Ashley." Kevin's voice floated up from the kitchen. "Let's move it. You're going to be late for school!"

"Come on." Mary-Kate grabbed her sister's arm and dragged her away from the mirror. "You know how Dad is when breakfast gets cold."

"But it's always cornflakes," Ashley protested, tossing the mascara on her dresser top. "They're *supposed* to be cold!"

The twins entered the kitchen just as their father was placing a plate of blueberry muffins on the table.

"Blueberry muffins!" Mary-Kate exclaimed. Kevin baked muffins only on special occasions. "Is this all for us?"

Kevin took off the apron he wore over his Oxford shirt and jeans. "No. I'm having some friends over after you leave. Try not to dirty the silverware," he joked.

"Funny, Dad," Ashley said.

Mary-Kate studied the plate of muffins. She selected one, then picked up her milk glass.

Kevin set the butter dish on the table, then stopped and stared at Ashley. "Honey, are you feeling okay?"

"Sure, Dad," Ashley asked. She grabbed a muffin and dropped it on her plate. "Why?"

"You look a little flushed," he said.

Mary-Kate nearly choked on her milk. "You mean *blushed*, Dad! Ashley— ow!" She broke off as Ashley kicked her under the table.

"Ashley, are you wearing make-up?" Kevin asked

with a frown. "You know my rules about make-up."

Mary-Kate gave her sister an "I told you so" look.

"But, Dad!" Ashley exclaimed. "I'm eleven!"

Kevin nodded. "That's right. And when you're thirteen you can wear make-up."

"Thirteen?" Ashley cried. "That's ages from now."

Kevin pointed up the stairs. "I want that stuff off before you go to school."

Ashley stood up and sighed. "Okay . . . but you can't stop the march of time."

"You're right," Kevin said. Then he pointed up the stairs again. "So . . . march!"

As Ashley plodded up the stairs, Mary-Kate raised her eyebrows at her father. "Dad, I think we're going to have trouble with Ashley," she remarked. She took a big bite of her muffin.

There was a knock on the door. "Come in," she called with her mouth full.

The door opened. Max and Jessica, the twins' friends, strolled into the kitchen.

"Hi," Jessica said.

"Hrrumph," Max grunted sleepily.

Mary-Kate studied her friends' back-to-school outfits. Jessica wore a new striped sweater and a pair of stretchy black jeans. Her long brown hair was pulled into a ponytail. And Mary-Kate wasn't positive, but she *thought* Jessica was wearing mascara.

Max's back-to-school clothes looked more like back-to-bed clothes. His baggy jeans were creased and his shirt was decorated with a jam stain. His short black hair stuck up in bunches on his head, as if he hadn't combed it.

"Hey, Jessica, Max," Kevin said cheerily. "All psyched for the first day of school?"

Max stared at Kevin as if he were from outer space.

"Oh, yeah, I'm pumped," he grumbled. "Instead of playing ball all day, I get to study Guatemala."

Kevin's eyes lit up. "How exciting! Guatemala has one of the most unusual ecosystems in the world," he said excitedly. "Did you know— "

Mary-Kate rolled her eyes. It was bad enough that their dad lectured *them* – but did he have to torture their friends, too?

"Dad, please," she begged. "Summer vacation doesn't end for another twenty minutes."

"Yeah," Max agreed. He reached over Mary-Kate's shoulder for a blueberry muffin. "And I kind of like to ease my way into the whole learning thing.

So my body doesn't go into shock."

Kevin looked blank. "Shock?" he repeated.

Jessica nodded. "Last year Max opened his maths book early and threw up."

Max shrugged. "I have a condition."

Kevin started to turn towards the stove. Then he stopped and gave Jessica a second look.

"Jessica?" he asked slowly. "Are you wearing make-up?"

Mary-Kate stopped chewing. Did her dad have a lip-gloss radar under the table, or what?

Jessica nodded excitedly. "Yeah. Everybody's doing it for the first day of school."

"Not everybody," Mary-Kate chimed in. She pointed to Ashley as her sister trudged down the stairs. Her face was freshly scrubbed and free of make-up.

"Ashley!" Jessica exclaimed. "I thought you were going to wear make-up today."

Ashley gave her dad a quick glare.

"So did I," she muttered. She waved her hand towards the door. "Come on, you guys. We don't want to be late for school."

Ashley and Mary-Kate grabbed their lunches and some more muffins. They kissed their father.

"Bye, Dad," Ashley said.

17

"See you," Mary-Kate called.

Kevin followed the twins as they headed for the door.

"By the way, girls," he said, "I'm putting up some fliers at the university today."

"Fliers?" Ashley repeated.

"What kind of fliers?" Mary-Kate asked. Her eyes lit up. "Are we finally getting a dog?"

Kevin shook his head. "I need a babysitter for you girls on the days I teach late."

Mary-Kate froze. "A *babysitter*?" She couldn't believe her ears.

A babysitter at the age of eleven was the ultimate humiliation. Like carrying a lunch box to school. Or drinking out of a juice box!

So that was the reason for the blueberry muffins. They were a bribe!

"Babysitters are for babies, Dad," Ashley complained.

"You know, you're right," Kevin said.

Mary-Kate and Ashley exchanged hopeful glances.

"So instead," Kevin cracked a smile, "I'll hire a pre-teen activities coordinator."

Mary-Kate glared at her father. How could he joke at a time like this? "Call it what you want, Dad.

It's still a babysitter."

Kevin straightened his tie. "I'm going to have Mrs. Baker watch you after school until I find someone permanent," he said.

"Mrs. Baker?" Mary-Kate gasped.

"But she's so old!" Ashley protested.

"She's very professional," Kevin added. "She's babysat for years."

"Yeah," Mary-Kate grumbled. "Probably for Abraham Lincoln."

"Wait. You guys still need a *babysitter?*" Max asked.

Mary-Kate grabbed the blueberry muffin from Max's hand. "Don't make me hurt you," she warned.

"Oooh, somebody's having a bad day," Jessica murmured.

"Big surprise," Mary-Kate grumbled as she walked out the door. "It's the first day of school, and Mrs. Baker is our babysitter. Can this day get any *worse?*"

CHAPTER THREE

"The earth has always had some kind of greenhouse effect to keep the air warm," Kevin Burke explained to his class. He pointed to a map of the world. "But if it gets any warmer, the ice will melt, the oceans will rise – and you'll be surfing to school."

Kevin was a professor of environmental studies. That morning he was teaching a large college class about global warming.

"That's all for today. Now remember," he said. "Wednesday morning we meet in the lab at seven-thirty sharp."

The students stood up and gathered their books. Kevin was just about to return to his desk when a girl in the second row waved her arms in the air.

"Attention, everybody!" she called out.

Kevin glanced up at the girl. She wore a short, tight, brown skirt and a tie-dyed shirt. Her very bright red hair was cut in layers. He wondered if it was dyed.

"Is something wrong?" he asked.

The girl shook her head and began to clap. "I just want to say what a great class this was. Thank you, Professor Burke!"

She motioned to the other students to join in. Soon the whole classroom rang with applause.

Kevin smiled. But as he took a bow, he couldn't help wondering: *Exactly what is this girl up to? The class was good – but it wasn't* that *good!*

"Thank you very much," he said, feeling a little flustered. "And thank you, Miss . . ."

"Moore," the girl said. "Carrie Moore." The rest of the class gathered their books and began to leave. The girl continued, "Professor, before I go, I have one little question about the Wednesday lab."

Here it comes, Kevin thought. "Yes?" he asked.

Carrie's five-inch platform shoes clunked as she walked to the front of the class.

"Seven-thirty?" she shouted as she reached his desk. "Are you nuts? That puts me at breakfast at six-fifteen. It's still dark!"

"Sorry, Carrie," Kevin said firmly. He began packing his books. "But that's when the lab is scheduled."

"What if I see if the other professor can push his lab back to nine-thirty?" Carrie asked. "Then we can start at eight."

Kevin folded his arms. "I don't see why getting up early is such a problem."

"You would if you spent the last year working as a card dealer in Las Vegas," Carrie said. "Lots of late nights there."

"A card dealer? Las Vegas?" Kevin exclaimed. "How old are you, anyway?"

"Twenty-six," Carrie replied. "I took a little time off from college to see the world. Now I'm back."

"Well, the first thing you're going to learn is how to get up early," Kevin said with a smile. He picked up his briefcase.

"You're the boss," Carrie said. As she turned towards the door she glanced over her shoulder. "By the way – who's *your* boss?"

Kevin folded his arms across his chest. "You know, every year I have one student that I know I'll remember for the rest of my life," he said. He sighed. "This year I have a feeling it's you."

CHAPTER FOUR

"I can't believe Miss Tandy gave us homework on the first day of school," Mary-Kate complained.

"You got Tandy?" Max asked. He shook his head. "I heard she gives homework to kids who aren't even in her class!"

The twins sat with Max on the front stoop of their brownstone house. They had all survived the first day of school. Now they had to survive the first day of homework!

"No way am I missing our softball game next Monday just because I have to do homework," Mary-Kate said.

Ashley slumped so low her chin almost hit the ground. Baseball talk always made her feel left out.

Mary-Kate was a real pro. She was great at hitting, catching – even arguing with the umpire!

The only thing I'm good at, Ashley thought, *is warming the bench.*

Ashley knew she was good at other things, like cooking and baking. But no one cheered your name or carried you on their shoulders for making a perfect chocolate chip cookie.

"Do you really think we can beat those kids from Dearborn Street?" Max asked Mary-Kate.

"We'd better," Mary-Kate declared. "I've been ragging them about it for three weeks."

"And they've been chasing *me* home because they think I'm you," Ashley complained.

"Sorry about that." Mary-Kate giggled.

Ashley heard the door to the house open. Turning around, she saw Mrs. Baker in the doorway, holding two jackets.

"It's the warden," Mary-Kate whispered.

"Shh," Ashley warned. "She'll hear you."

"Mary-Kate, Ashley," Mrs. Baker said. "It's getting chilly. You'd better put on your jackets."

"But I'm not cold, Mrs. Baker," Mary-Kate argued.

"Neither am I," Ashley said.

Mrs. Baker stared down her nose at the twins.

"Well," she said. "You can always come inside."

Ashley rolled her eyes. She and Mary-Kate quickly reached for their jackets.

"I thought that might change your minds," Mrs. Baker said cheerfully. She waited until the girls buttoned up their jackets. Then she turned and walked – slowly – back into the house.

"I can't believe Mrs. Baker is your babysitter," Max whispered. "She's so old, I'll bet her bedtime is before yours."

"She can't even tell us apart," Ashley complained. "She wants us to wear name tags!"

"Well, she's not going to be our babysitter for long," Mary-Kate declared. "I've decided we're not having one this year."

Ashley stared at her sister. "Are you for real, Mary-Kate? Try telling that to Dad."

"Dad doesn't have to know." Mary-Kate tapped her forehead with her finger. "I have a plan."

"What plan?" Max asked, his eyes wide.

"I'm still working on the details," Mary-Kate admitted. "But I'll come up with something."

"Hey, guys," a voice called out.

Ashley glanced up. A red-haired young woman in jeans and platform sandals was studying the house.

"Wow!" Ashley whispered to Mary-Kate. "Look at her clothes. Now *that's* what I call style."

"Do you think that's her real hair colour?" Mary-Kate whispered back.

The young woman stepped up to the twins. "Is this two thirty-eight Belmont?" she asked.

"Why?" Mary-Kate shot back. "Are you a cop?"

"Nope," the woman said with a smile. "My name is Carrie, and I'm here to apply for the babysitting job. I saw your dad's flier hanging up at school."

Ashley bolted upright. Uh-oh. The *B* word!

"Too late," Mary-Kate said quickly. "The position was just filled."

Ashley hid a grin. She could always count on Mary-Kate to think fast!

"Oh, no!" Carrie looked disappointed.

Mary-Kate shrugged. "Sorry."

"I guess it's not your day," Ashley told Carrie, playing along. "But if you'd like to leave your phone number, we'll give it to our dad. He should be home in a couple of minutes."

Carrie's eyes narrowed.

"Really?" she asked. "But if your dad's not home yet, how did he hire a babysitter already?"

Whoops! Ashley felt her cheeks turn red.

Max leaned back on the steps and laughed.

"Oooh!" he cried. "Busted!"

Mary-Kate glared at him. "Hey, Max," she said through gritted teeth. "Somebody wants you across the street."

"Oh, yeah?" Max asked. He stretched his neck and peered across the street. "Who?"

"Me!" Mary-Kate snapped.

"Okay, okay," Max said. He jumped up from the steps and grabbed his books. "I'm out of here."

Carrie chuckled as Max ran down the block. Then she sat down on the steps next to the twins.

"Hey, I can understand why you guys don't want somebody watching you all the time," she said. "You've got a lot of stuff on your minds – school, hair, clothes, boys."

Ashley grinned at Mary-Kate. "She knows me so well."

"Clothes, boys – big deal!" Mary-Kate said in a disgusted voice. "Unless she can teach me to throw a knuckleball, I don't think she's babysitter material at all."

"I can't do that," Carrie said. "But I can show you a mean slider I learned at Fantasy Baseball Camp."

Mary-Kate's eyes widened.

"You went to baseball camp?" she cried. "Did you like it?"

"Are you kidding?" Carrie cried. "One girl and twenty-two guys. What's not to like?"

"What else do you like to do?" Ashley asked Carrie. "You know. Besides baseball."

Carrie began counting on her fingers. "Let's see. I like to listen to CDs, see as many movies as I can . . . and shop."

"Did you say *shop*?" Ashley asked. Her eyes opened wide. Now they were getting somewhere!

"Oh, sure," Carrie said. She wiggled her platform sandals in front of her. "In fact, I wish I were a centipede so I'd have an excuse to buy more shoes."

Ashley laughed. She still didn't want a babysitter – but if they had to have one, Carrie wouldn't be so bad!

"Carrie?" Mary-Kate asked. "Will you teach me how to slide into first base?"

"Will you lend me some of your clothes?" Ashley asked, wiggling closer to Carrie.

"Whoa!" Carrie laughed, holding up her hands. "I didn't get the job yet."

"Girls, I'm home!" Kevin called as he walked up the block.

"Leave it to us," Ashley whispered confidently. "The job is yours – trust me!"

CHAPTER FIVE

As Kevin walked down the street, he saw Mary-Kate and Ashley running towards him.

"Dad, Dad!" Ashley called. "We found the perfect person to watch us after school!"

"Yeah, she's great!" Mary-Kate agreed. "She can play baseball with me and go shopping with Ashley!"

Kevin raised his eyebrows. "Somebody you *both* like?" he asked. "Maybe I'll marry her."

He glanced at the young woman who stood by his stoop.

Then he stared. It was Carrie Moore!

"Professor Burke," she said, sounding surprised.

"Then again, maybe I *won't* marry her," Kevin

muttered to himself. He couldn't believe it. He wanted to hire a babysitter – not someone who *needed* a babysitter! Carrie was so wrong for the job!

Carrie unfolded the bright pink paper and waved it in the air. "I had no clue this was your flier, Professor Burke."

"I guess it's a small world," Kevin managed. Too small!

"Time out." Mary-Kate formed a *T* with her hands. "Do you two know each other or something?"

"Yeah," Ashley asked, wrinkling her nose. "Are you, like . . . friends?"

Kevin felt his face grow red. He opened his mouth to protest. But Carrie beat him to it.

"I'm in one of your dad's classes," she explained.

Ashley burst out laughing. "You mean our dad's your teacher?"

"Did he give you homework on your first day, too?" Mary-Kate asked with a wicked grin.

Kevin reached over and ruffled Mary-Kate's hair. Time for a little privacy.

"Why don't you girls wash up for dinner while I talk to Carrie?" he suggested.

"Sure, Dad," Ashley said. She smiled at Carrie and waved. "Bye, Carrie."

"Hope we'll see you soon," Mary-Kate said. She gave her father the thumbs-up sign. "Really soon."

Kevin watched his daughters run into the house. They seemed to like Carrie a lot.

If only he felt the same way!

"This is the perfect job for me, Professor Burke," Carrie said confidently. "Your house is close to the college, and your girls are great. Besides, I'm much too old to flip burgers."

"Carrie— " Kevin started to say.

Carrie rubbed her hands together. "So when do I start?"

"St-start?" Kevin stammered.

Uh-oh. How was he going to tell Carrie that she was a definite no-go?

"Carrie, I just put up the flier this morning," he said at last. "I want to meet more people. Tell you what – I'll call you."

Carrie gave him a long look. "No, you won't," she said.

Kevin raised his eyebrows. "Excuse me?"

"Professor, the last guy who told me 'I'll call you' was Bobby Clayton in junior high," Carrie told him. She cracked a little smile. "I think I'm going to hear from Bobby before I hear from you."

Walking away, she called over her shoulder,

"Good luck, Professor Burke. I hope you find someone great."

Kevin took a deep breath. *That wasn't easy. But I made the right decision*, he thought as he turned towards the house.

Then he glanced up and saw Mary-Kate and Ashley, their noses pressed against their window.

He stopped in his tracks.

Or . . . did I? he asked himself.

CHAPTER SIX

"Are you taking all that stuff up to the attic?" Kevin asked as he walked into the kitchen the next afternoon.

"It's just a little snack," Mary-Kate said.

Kevin peered into the picnic basket they were packing. It was filled with cookies, pretzels, crisps, and a jumbo bottle of soda. A junk food feast!

"Who are you feeding up there?" he asked. "The Chicago Cubs?"

"Funny you should mention baseball, Dad," Mary-Kate said. "Max, Jessica, and Brian are upstairs. We're having a strategy meeting about the big softball game next Monday."

Ashley lifted the picnic basket off the counter.

33

"My strategy is not to play," she announced.

As the twins headed for the stairs, Kevin took a deep breath.

I've waited long enough. It's now or never, he told himself.

Here goes . . .

"Oh, by the way," he called, trying to make his voice sound casual. "I hired Mrs. Baker to watch you girls after school permanently."

Mary-Kate and Ashley stopped short. They turned and stared in disbelief.

"Mrs. Baker?" Mary-Kate cried. "But she's *ancient!*"

"Yeah," Ashley agreed. "We can't even talk to her. She's, like – from the Middle Ages."

"What happened to Carrie?" Mary-Kate asked.

"She was so cool," Ashley added.

"That's the problem," Kevin said. "Carrie was a little *too* cool. I need someone more responsible to watch you after school. A bit less . . . flaky."

"Carrie's not flaky," Ashley said. "She's funny. Like Mom was."

"Yeah." Mary-Kate nodded. "Carrie even likes sports and shopping, just like Mom did."

"Your mom?" Kevin raised his eyebrows. Come to think of it, Carrie did kind of remind him of . . .

34

Wait a minute – what was he thinking?

Back to business. "Okay," Kevin said. "How about this? Carrie will be the first runner-up. If Mrs. Baker can't fulfil her role as babysitter, then Carrie will step in."

Mary-Kate sighed. "In other words, forget it."

The girls trudged out of the kitchen.

"Just give Mrs. Baker a chance," Kevin called. "I heard she used to babysit for Leonardo DiCaprio!"

The kitchen door closed with a loud slam.

"Nah," he said to himself. "I didn't think they'd buy that."

"Hi, guys," Mary-Kate said as she and Ashley walked into the attic.

The attic was the twins' own private hangout. There was a big lumpy sofa and a colourful rug on the floor. Posters of rock stars and athletes covered the walls. There was even a telescope next to the window for stargazing. Or neighbour-gazing.

"Yo!" their friend Brian greeted them. He, Max, and Jessica were busy shooting Nerf hoops.

"Bad news," Ashley said. She placed the snack basket on a small table. "Dad hired Mrs. Baker to watch us after school permanently."

"What happened to Carrie?" Jessica asked.

"She's history," Ashley said. "Unless something happens to Mrs. Baker."

"No problem," Brian said. He whacked his palm with his fist. "I know some pretty tough guys in the seventh grade."

"Brian, you idiot," Mary-Kate snapped. She gave Brian a smack on his head. "We don't want to hurt her. We just want her to find something else to do, so she doesn't have time to watch us. Then our dad will hire Carrie."

"Let's all think of something," Ashley suggested.

"Sure," Max said. He plopped down next to the snacks. "But not on an empty stomach."

Soon the only sound in the attic was munching, crunching, and slurping. Mary-Kate grinned. That must mean her friends were thinking hard.

Suddenly Jessica jumped up.

"I know!" she said. "Why don't you get Mrs. Baker a job?"

"A job?" Ashley asked. "Where?"

"Fast-food places hire senior citizens," Jessica pointed out.

"Yeah," Max groaned. "That's when it becomes slow food."

"Guys, can we please concentrate?" Ashley begged. "We've got to think of something."

"If I think any harder, my brain will explode!" Max complained.

"What brain?" Brian joked.

The kids went back to thinking. Then Brian jumped up and snapped his fingers.

"I've got it!" he cried.

"What?" everyone asked at once.

"You know when my mom gets off my back?" Brian asked. "When she has a boyfriend!"

Mary-Kate knew that Brian's mom was divorced and liked to go on dates – but she was also thirty years younger than Mrs. Baker!

"Who's going to want to go out with a seventy-year-old lady?" Mary-Kate asked.

The attic was so quiet you could hear a pin drop.

Then Ashley broke the silence.

"How about a seventy-year-old man?" she suggested.

Max snorted. "Where are we going to find a seventy-year-old man?" he asked.

It was as if a lightbulb suddenly flashed inside Mary-Kate's head. Jumping up, she ran to the telescope by the window.

"Mary-Kate, are you spying on our neighbours again?" Ashley asked.

"Nope," Mary-Kate replied. "I'm just doing research."

"Research?" Ashley repeated.

Mary-Kate aimed the telescope out the window and moved it back and forth slowly.

"What do you see?" Jessica asked.

Mary-Kate scanned every inch of Belmont Street.

"I spy with my little eye . . . a boy walking a golden retriever . . . a grocery truck . . . an old man getting his mail— "

Mary-Kate gasped. She pressed her eye against the telescope for a closer look. The bald, elderly man getting his mail was Mr. Fillmore, from down the street. He wore a woollen waistcoat over a checked shirt.

"Mr. Fillmore. Of course," Mary-Kate breathed. He was the perfect match!

CHAPTER SEVEN

"All systems go," Ashley reported to Mary-Kate.

It was later that afternoon. The twins stood outside their house. They were about to put their matchmaking plan into action.

"Okay, I got Mr. Fillmore," Mary-Kate whispered to Ashley. "You throw some fairy dust on Mrs. Baker."

Ashley glanced up at Mrs. Baker. The white-haired babysitter sat on a chair at the top of the Burkes' stoop. She was knitting something – probably more warm sweaters for the twins.

"Check," Ashley said.

Two houses away, Mr. Fillmore was sweeping the sidewalk in front of his steps. Mary-Kate walked over to him and gave him a long, hard stare.

Mr. Fillmore looked up from his broom. "Something wrong, Mary-Kate?" he asked.

"Sorry for staring, Mr. Fillmore," Mary-Kate said. "But I just don't see it."

"See what?" Mr. Fillmore asked.

"Mrs. Baker said you look like a movie star," Mary-Kate said. "But it's probably just because she's in love with you."

Mr. Fillmore gripped the broom handle. He leaned over to Mary-Kate. "Did you say . . . in love?" he asked. "With me?"

Mary-Kate nodded. "Don't look now. But she's staring at you."

Mr. Fillmore glanced up quickly. Mrs. Baker was bent over her knitting.

"She turned away," Mary-Kate said. "I told you not to look."

Down the street, Ashley watched the scene closely. She nodded to herself. It was her turn now!

She sat down beside Mrs. Baker. "Poor Mary-Kate," she said.

"What's wrong with Mary-Kate, dear?" Mrs. Baker asked. Her eyes were still on her knitting.

"Mr. Fillmore is pumping her for information about you again," Ashley explained.

Mrs. Baker looked up from her knitting.

"Gracious!" she exclaimed. "Why would he do that?"

"Everyone knows he's got a major crush on you," Ashley said with a sly smile. "Why do you think he's always staring at you?"

"That's funny." Mrs. Baker frowned. "I've never seen him stare at me before."

"That's because he always turns away when you look at him," Ashley explained.

"Is that right?" Mrs. Baker's cheeks turned pink. She peered at Mr. Fillmore.

Ashley followed the babysitter's gaze down the street. Sure enough, Mr. Fillmore was staring at Mrs. Baker. *Good work, Mary-Kate!* Ashley cheered silently.

Mrs. Baker giggled as he quickly turned away. "He *was* looking at me, Ashley!"

"Would I lie to you?" Ashley asked with a grin.

"You're right, Mary-Kate! She *was* looking at me!" Mr. Fillmore exclaimed, two houses away.

Yes! Mary-Kate thought excitedly. *Now on to the next step.*

"Um, Mr. Fillmore," she said. "Maybe you should ask Mrs. Baker on a date. I hear the Sizzler's got a great early-bird special."

Mr. Fillmore scratched his chin. "Early bird, huh?" He leaned towards Mary-Kate. "I do kind of like their Malibu Chicken," he admitted with a grin.

"And Mrs. Baker's a freak for the salad bar," Mary-Kate said. She gave Mr. Fillmore a light slap on the back. "Go get her!"

Mr. Fillmore turned towards Mrs. Baker.

"Wait!" Mary-Kate held out her hand. "Lose the broom."

Mr. Fillmore handed the broom to Mary-Kate. Then he threw back his shoulders and strutted towards Mrs. Baker.

"Ah!" Mary-Kate sighed. She leaned against the broom and smiled. "Isn't love grand?"

The first part of the plan went off without a hitch.

Now for the second part – getting their dad to hire Carrie!

CHAPTER EIGHT

"But Mrs. Baker, I don't understand," Kevin protested. He stood in the centre of the living room, shaking his head. "Two days ago you were thrilled to get this job."

Mrs. Baker clutched her handbag. She wore a brand-new cardigan sweater – and brand-new red lipstick.

"Two days ago, making tuna sandwiches was the highlight of my life," she said. She straightened her shoulders and smiled. "Now I have a *boyfriend*!"

Mary-Kate gave Ashley a slight nudge.

"But, Mrs. Baker," Kevin begged. "I only need you for a little while in the afternoon."

Mrs. Baker shook her head. "Sorry, but those are

43

Henry's best hours."

"Henry?" Kevin asked.

"Mr. Fillmore, Dad," Ashley whispered.

Kevin's eyes widened. "Oh!"

Mary-Kate jumped up from the sofa. She gave Mrs. Baker a big hug. "Oh, Mrs. Baker," she said. "I'm going to miss you so much. Do you really have to leave?"

Ashley hid a grin. Mary-Kate was really laying it on thick!

"Yes, I do," Mrs. Baker said. "But you can visit me at Mr. Fillmore's any time, dear."

"Is there anything I can do to make you reconsider, Mrs. Baker?" Kevin asked. "More . . . money?"

Ashley gulped. Her dad had just said the magic word. Would Mrs. Baker change her mind and choose money over love?

But Mrs. Baker shook her head. "I've made my decision," she said firmly. "Now if you'll excuse me, Henry and I have plans. It's senior night at the racetrack."

A moment later the twins watched as Mrs. Baker left their house – for good.

Kevin heaved a big sigh. "I guess we're back to square one now," he said.

Ashley jumped up. "Wait a minute, Dad," she

said. "Didn't you have a second choice? What's her name? Mary? Terry? Cherie?"

Kevin was about to speak when the doorbell rang. Mary-Kate and Ashley followed their dad to the door.

When Kevin opened the door, his jaw dropped.

"Carrie!" he exclaimed.

"That's it," Ashley said. She was doing her best not to laugh. *"Carrie!"*

"Hi, Professor Burke," Carrie said. "You called?"

"I-I did?" Kevin stammered.

"Actually, Ashley was the one who called," Carrie said. "But she gave me your message."

Kevin glanced down at Ashley. His eyes narrowed.

"Why, thank you, Ashley," he said. "So you can read my mind, huh?"

Ashley shrugged. "I guess so."

Kevin stepped towards her. "Can you read my mind now?"

Ashley gulped. What she read was – trouble!

"Come on, Dad." Mary-Kate came to her sister's rescue. "Ashley was only trying to help. Besides, Carrie was your first runner-up. Remember?"

"So she was," Kevin muttered. He shook his head slightly, then turned back to Carrie. "Looks like you're hired."

45

"Yes!" Mary-Kate cheered under her breath.

"Ashley?" Kevin asked. "Since you seem to be in charge here, how much am I paying her?"

Ashley grinned. "Carrie and I are still negotiating."

"But don't worry, Professor Burke," Carrie added. "Ashley's offer was quite fair."

The twins laughed and gave each other high fives.

They had just lost a babysitter – and gained a cool new friend!

CHAPTER NINE

"So let me get this straight," Carrie said, pouring milk into the twins' glasses. "You two can read each other's minds?"

"Sometimes. Sort of," Mary-Kate said. "It's a twin thing."

"But don't worry, Carrie," Ashley said. She took a gulp of milk. "We're not passing any secret messages or anything. We're going to be perfect angels today!"

"Why today?" Carrie asked. She sat down at the kitchen table between the twins.

"Because we don't want you to quit on your first day." Mary-Kate gave Ashley a little wink. "Like all our other babysitters."

"What?" Carrie gasped.

"Only kidding!" Mary-Kate said, laughing.

It was three-thirty. She and Ashley had rushed home from school to spend the afternoon with Carrie.

"So, what are we going to do today?" Ashley asked Carrie. "Go to the mall?"

"No way!" Mary-Kate protested. "Carrie is going to teach me how to throw a knuckleball. Right, Carrie?"

"I'm sorry to disappoint both of you," Carrie said. "But we're not practising throws or shopping."

"Then what?" Mary-Kate asked. Maybe Carrie had something even better in mind. Like in-line skating. Or looking at baseball cards.

"You're doing your homework," Carrie said.

"Homework?" Mary-Kate cried.

This was what they rushed home for?

"We usually do our homework *after* dinner," Ashley said. "Between TV shows."

"Look, guys," Carrie said. "I know homework can sometimes be a drag, but isn't it better to get it out of the way? Then you'll have the rest of the day to have fun."

Maybe she's right, Mary-Kate thought. *I never*

thought of it that way before.

The phone rang. Mary-Kate ran to answer it.

"Hi, Mary-Kate." Her father's voice came over the line.

"Hey, Dad!" Mary-Kate answered. She could never figure out how their dad could tell her voice apart from Ashley's on the phone!

"How's everything going with Carrie?" Kevin asked.

"Great, Dad," Mary-Kate said. She moved the receiver closer to her mouth and whispered, "Guess what? She thinks homework is a drag, too. Just like me!"

"A drag?" Kevin's voice sounded disapproving. "Is that what she told you? I want to speak to her right now."

Whoops! I shouldn't have said that, Mary-Kate realised. *He's taking it the wrong way.*

"Calm down, Dad," she said. "Carrie's cool."

"But— "

"Uh-oh, got to go. See you, Dad," Mary-Kate said quickly. "Love you!" She hung up the phone and ran back to the table.

"Now," Carrie said. She folded her hands on the table. "What homework do you have today?"

"The usual," Ashley said. "Maths, history,

English, and some extra-credit work."

"Extra credit?" Mary-Kate made a face. "That's where I draw the line. When the homework's done, it's time to quit."

"Quit?" Carrie asked. "Mary-Kate, if you were in a softball game and your team was way ahead, would you throw down your bat and quit?"

"Are we talking about baseball again?" Ashley groaned.

Carrie leaned towards Mary-Kate and looked her in the eye. "Well? Would you?"

"No," Mary-Kate said, shaking her head. "We'd keep on going. So we'd win with the highest score possible."

"Exactly!" Carrie said. "That's what extra credit is all about. Getting as many points as you can, even after you know you're ahead."

"Oh!" Mary-Kate said. Hmmm. Maybe Carrie had something there.

"Mary-Kate Burke isn't a quitter, is she?" Carrie asked.

"No way!" Mary-Kate declared.

Carrie waved a fist in the air. "Then what do you say we crack those books and rack up some extra credit?"

Mary-Kate shrugged. "Okay, okay. I guess

you talked me into it."

"Wow!" Ashley exclaimed. "My sister – doing extra credit! I never thought I'd live to see the day!"

Mary-Kate froze with her pencil in midair.

Hey, that's right! she thought. I'm *doing extra credit?*

She stared at Carrie in amazement.

What will she have us doing next?

CHAPTER TEN

"Okay, that's it for today," Kevin told his class. "Next time, a little field trip. We'll go to the top of the Sears Tower – the tallest building in Chicago – and learn about gravity." He grinned. "Didn't I tell you I would bring science to new heights?"

The students laughed as they stood up to leave.

"See you later, Professor Burke," Carrie called.

Kevin frowned and motioned Carrie over. *Does she remember what tonight is?* he wondered.

"Carrie, wait," he said. "It's Thursday night. Do you know what that means?"

Carrie thought it over.

"Yeah," she said. "Not my favourite TV night."

Kevin shook his head. He knew it was Carrie's

first week on the job – but she still had a lot to learn.

"This is the night I teach late," he reminded her. "I won't be home until nine o'clock."

"Nine," Carrie said, nodding. "Got it."

She turned and headed for the door.

"Wait, wait!" Kevin called.

"Now what?" Carrie asked.

"The girls have a routine, and I need you to stick to it," Kevin explained. "You've got to make sure they get to bed by nine o'clock sharp."

"Okay," Carrie said. "But that hardly gives me time to pierce Mary-Kate's nose."

Kevin froze. *Pierce Mary-Kate's nose?* Was she serious?

"That's okay." Carrie gave him a wicked grin. "I guess I can do it while she's asleep."

That night after dinner Ashley decided to bake a batch of her special chocolate chip cookies. She wanted to celebrate Carrie's first week on the job.

"These smell awesome," Carrie said. She scooped the hot cookies off a baking sheet and placed them carefully on a cooling rack. "Who taught you how to make them, Ashley?"

Ashley smiled as she pulled another batch of cookies from the oven. "My mom," she said. "She was absolutely the best baker ever."

Carrie leaned against the counter. "When did she die?"

Ashley felt a pang of sadness. "When we were in third grade. Dad says I got her cooking talent. Mary-Kate got her jump shot."

At that moment Mary-Kate walked into the kitchen, talking into a cordless phone. Ashley could tell from her twin's face that she was tense.

"Uh-oh," Carrie whispered to Ashley. "It looks serious."

"It *must* be serious," Ashley whispered back. "She walked right past the cookies."

"I don't care if you're hurt, Brian," Mary-Kate said into the phone. "You're our clean-up hitter. Haven't you heard of playing through the pain?"

Ashley and Carrie exchanged puzzled glances.

A second later Mary-Kate jabbed the OFF button on the phone. "That Brian is such a wimp!" she cried.

"How come?" Ashley asked. She picked up a warm cookie.

"He broke his leg," Mary-Kate said, disgusted.

"Ouch," Carrie commented.

"It's only one leg!" Mary-Kate exclaimed. "I don't see why he can't still play on Monday."

"Tough luck, kiddo," Carrie said. She popped a chocolate chip cookie into Mary-Kate's mouth.

"Who are you going to get to replace him?" Ashley asked.

"I don't know." Mary-Kate grabbed another cookie.

Ashley was about to remove more freshly baked cookies from the pan, when she caught Mary-Kate staring at her. Her sister's eyes narrowed thoughtfully. She began to chew faster and faster.

Oh, no, Ashley thought. It was all too easy to read her sister's mind. Mary-Kate was getting a brainstorm – and Ashley knew what it was!

Mary-Kate tilted her head as she studied Ashley. "Ashley, pick up that rolling pin and hold it like a baseball bat."

"I knew it!" Ashley yanked off her oven mitt and slammed it on the counter. "You want me to replace Brian, don't you?"

Mary-Kate grabbed Ashley by the shoulders.

"You're going to play, Ashley," she declared.

Ashley felt her stomach turn over.

"I am not!" she said. "And you're spitting cookie crumbs all over me!"

"What's the problem, Ashley?" Carrie asked. "Why don't you want to play?"

"Because I stink," Ashley said. "All the kids will see that I can't hit."

"They already know you can't hit," Mary-Kate declared.

"Gee, thanks!" Ashley muttered. Why didn't they just throw her to the sharks? It would be a lot kinder than making her play softball.

Then she felt Carrie's hand on her shoulder.

"Hey, anybody can hit," Carrie said. "Even you."

Ashley looked doubtfully at Carrie. "You've never seen me at bat."

Carrie walked to the coat rack and grabbed her jacket. "Come on. I know a place where you can pick up some great tips."

"Where are we going?" Ashley asked.

"To watch a Cubs game," Carrie said.

Mary-Kate gasped. "A real Cubs game? Like, the Major League team?"

Carrie threw the girls their jackets. "Of course, a real Cubs game."

"Right now?" Ashley asked, amazed.

"Right now!" Carrie confirmed, smiling.

Wow! Ashley thought. *Carrie sure didn't waste any time!*

She pulled her jacket on slowly. Something about this didn't seem right.

"Shouldn't we let Dad know that we're going?" she asked.

Carrie shook her head. "He's in the middle of a class right now. Besides, we'll get home way before he does."

"Come on, Ashley," Mary-Kate said. "Don't you want to see a real Cubs game?"

"Sure," Ashley said. "As long as we're just going to watch."

Mary-Kate planted her hands on her hips. "I doubt the Chicago Cubs will recruit you for their team."

"Ready?" Carrie asked.

Mary-Kate grabbed another handful of Ashley's chocolate chip cookies.

"*Now* I'm ready!" she said with a grin.

"Here we are!" Carrie announced.

Mary-Kate and Ashley followed Carrie off the bus. They were on an ordinary block filled with ordinary buildings. "I don't see Wrigley Field anywhere," Mary-Kate said.

"Yeah," Ashley said, frowning. "I thought we were going to watch a Cubs game."

"We are," Carrie said. She smiled mysteriously.

The twins followed her to a brick building in the

middle of the block. It had a dark red awning over the door and two tall plants on each end of the doorstep. "This is where I live," Carrie announced.

What are we doing here? Ashley wondered. *What's going on?*

"We've never lived in an apartment building," Mary-Kate said as they walked into the lobby. It had a marble floor and two big mirrors on the wall.

Carrie laughed. "And I've never lived in a house."

"What's it like having so many neighbours?" Ashley asked.

Carrie pushed the elevator button. "When I was a kid it was neat. Especially on Hallowe'en," she told the twins. "We'd start on the first floor and trick-or-treat all the way up to the sixth floor. By the time we were finished we had tons of candy!"

The elevator came and they filed in. "Going up!" Carrie announced.

They rode all the way to the top floor. Then they climbed a small staircase leading to a heavy green door.

"Tah-daaaaah!" Carrie sang. She swung the door wide open.

Ashley felt a cool breeze. She stepped out slowly.

"Hey, wait a minute," she said, looking around.

"This is the roof. What are we doing up here?" Now she was *really* confused. And she wasn't crazy about heights either.

"Carrie." Mary-Kate's eyes opened wide. "Don't tell me you *live* up here!"

"Nah," Carrie said. She made a face. "Pigeons make terrible flatmates. My apartment is downstairs." She walked across the tar rooftop to a waist-high wall. "But I do kind of like the view," she added with a smile. "Check it out."

Carrie is definitely nuts, Ashley thought. She stole a nervous glance at Mary-Kate.

Mary-Kate didn't seem worried. She ran to the wall and peeked over.

"Wow!" she exclaimed.

What's down there? Ashley wondered. She followed her sister.

"Awesome!" she cried when she saw what Mary-Kate was staring at.

Right below them was Wrigley Field – and a real live Cubs game!

The bright stadium lamps seemed to light up the whole sky. From where Ashley stood, she could see practically everything.

"Is this great or what?" Carrie asked.

"Are you kidding?" Mary-Kate cried. "I can see

home plate from here!"

"I can smell the hot dogs!" Ashley said.

Carrie leaned against the wall and grinned.

"Take it from me, girls," she said. "When it comes to baseball, the best seat in the house . . . is on top of the house!"

Ashley smiled. She wasn't nervous any more.

Carrie isn't crazy, she realised.

She's just the coolest person ever!

CHAPTER ELEVEN

"Hi, Mrs. Lacy," Kevin Burke said into the phone. He paced back and forth in the kitchen. He couldn't remember a time when he was more frantic with worry. "Are my girls at your house?"

"No, they're not," Mrs. Lacy said. "Is there a problem?"

"No." Kevin felt a drop of sweat trickle down his forehead. "No, no problem. We got a new babysitter and there's been a little, uh, misunderstanding."

"Well, at least they're with their babysitter," Mrs. Lacy said. "That should make you feel better."

"Not quite," Kevin muttered. "I'll explain another day. Thanks, Mrs. Lacy."

He hung up the phone. His stomach was doing

triple flips. Where could Carrie have taken the twins? To a tattoo parlour? Bungee jumping?

He was about to dial again when he heard the front door open. He spun around and hurried into the living room. A wave of relief swept through his entire body.

Ashley and Mary-Kate stood there with Carrie. They were smiling, laughing, and talking nonstop.

"But how could I lose?" Mary-Kate said. "I had three aces and two kings."

"It still doesn't beat four of a kind," Carrie said.

Kevin cleared his throat.

"Hey, Dad," Mary-Kate said.

Ashley hugged her dad. "Dad, you wouldn't believe it. We had the coolest time!"

"We went to Carrie's apartment and watched a Cubs game," Mary-Kate added. "They were playing the Atlanta Braves."

"Carrie lives right across from Wrigley Field," Ashley explained. "We watched the whole thing from the roof."

"Is that so?" Kevin asked Carrie.

"And in between innings," Ashley added excitedly, "she taught us how to play poker!" She held up a deck of cards. "Feeling lucky, Dad?"

Kevin frowned. "Not right now," he said. "And

it's past your bedtime. Say goodnight to Carrie."

The twins smiled at Carrie.

"Goodnight, Carrie," Ashley said.

"See you," Mary-Kate said.

They kissed Kevin goodnight and hurried up the stairs.

As soon as he heard the bedroom door click shut, Kevin turned to Carrie. "Do you know what time it is?" he demanded.

Carrie checked her watch. "Ten past nine. But don't worry. The extra ten minutes are on me."

Kevin couldn't believe it. Carrie didn't have a clue about what she did wrong!

"Carrie, the girls were supposed to be in bed by nine o'clock!" he said, trying hard not to lose his temper.

"I know," Carrie said. "But we were having such a blast!"

"Well, I wasn't," Kevin snapped. "I come home to find my house empty, no message, and no note from their babysitter."

Carrie looked puzzled. "Sorry. But we were only ten minutes late."

"Ten minutes when I had no idea where my daughters were!" Kevin said, seething. "Do you have any idea how worried I was?"

"But you knew they were with me," Carrie said.

Kevin nodded. "Exactly!"

Carrie gave Kevin a reassuring smile. "Look, I understand you were worried. But once you get to know me better— "

"I don't plan on getting to know you better," Kevin interrupted.

Carrie froze.

"Are you . . . firing me?" she asked after a moment.

A million thoughts ran through Kevin's head. He knew that firing Carrie was the only thing to do . . . but what about the twins? Would he break their hearts? And what about Carrie? Would she push him off the Sears Tower tomorrow?

"Carrie, I need to know that my girls are in good hands," he said at last. "I don't get that from you."

"Professor Burke," Carrie said quickly. "About piercing Mary-Kate's nose. I would never— "

Kevin cut her off. "Goodnight, Carrie."

Carrie stared at him. Her eyes were full of hurt.

She turned and started towards the door.

"Say goodbye to the girls for me," she said over her shoulder.

Sure, Kevin thought. *If they ever speak to me again!*

CHAPTER TWELVE

Mary-Kate climbed into bed. "Do you think Dad will let me get a little tattoo just like Carrie's?" she asked Ashley.

Ashley giggled as she plumped up her pillow. The only tattoos she and Mary-Kate ever wore were the ones that peeled off! "Don't count on it," she advised.

Ashley fastened the top button of her silky pink pyjamas. Her sister was wearing her usual oversize Cubs T-shirt.

"Did the Cubs game change your mind about playing softball next Monday?" Mary-Kate asked her sister hopefully.

"No way," Ashley said. "But I had fun anyway."

The door to the twins' bedroom opened. Kevin walked in.

"Hey, Dad," Mary-Kate said.

"Hi," Kevin said. He sat down on the edge of Ashley's bed. "Listen, girls. About Carrie— "

"Is she neat or what?" Ashley interrupted.

"I'm not sure," Kevin said. "I know you like her, but I think she's a little too . . . loose with you girls."

Ashley laughed. "Too loose? She doesn't let us get away with *anything*!"

"Yeah," Mary-Kate agreed. "She makes me do my homework every day. She even had me doing extra credit."

Kevin raised his eyebrows. "But you told me that she said homework is a drag."

"She was just being honest." Ashley sat down on her own bed. "And she's not like a regular grown-up. We can talk to her about all kinds of stuff."

"What kind of stuff?" Kevin asked curiously.

Ashley gulped. She suddenly felt as if she had something in her mouth – like her own foot!

"Um . . . you know," she mumbled. "Things like music . . . clothes . . . movies . . . "

A mischievous grin spread across Mary-Kate's face.

"And Pokey Valentine!" she added.

Ashley grabbed her pillow and threw it at Mary-Kate. "That's private, Mary-Kate!" she protested.

Mary-Kate lay back on Ashley's pillow and giggled.

"Pokey Valentine?" Kevin asked. He wrinkled his nose. "What's a Pokey Valentine?"

Please, Mary-Kate, Ashley thought. *Don't... don't... don't...*

"Not what – who!" Mary-Kate hooted. "He's Ashley's boyfriend!"

Ashley's face turned as pink as her pyjamas. "He is not my boyfriend. He doesn't even know I like him!" she declared.

"He will tomorrow," Mary-Kate teased. Then she quickly ducked under her covers.

Ashley couldn't believe it. Her own twin sister – an informer!

"You're toast!" she screamed. She lunged at her sister.

But her dad caught her in midair. "Okay, okay," Kevin said. "Settle down. Both of you."

Mary-Kate pecked out from under her covers as Ashley sat back down.

"I didn't know you liked somebody, Ashley," Kevin said. He sounded a little hurt. "Why didn't you tell me about this Porky Valentine?"

"It's Pokey, not Porky," Ashley corrected. She stared down at her hands. "And the reason is . . . I don't know."

"But you told Carrie," Kevin pointed out.

Mary-Kate rolled her eyes. "Hello! Carrie is a girl."

Right, Ashley thought. No matter how great your dad was, you couldn't tell him *everything*. There was some stuff that you just had to talk to another girl about.

Kevin nodded slowly. "I see," he said. "So you'd rather talk to *her* about things like that."

"Well, yeah," Ashley said. "If Mom were still alive, we'd probably talk to her."

"But since she's not," Mary-Kate added, "Carrie can fill in. You know, sort of like a substitute."

Ashley watched as Kevin picked up a stuffed bear from her bed. He gazed down at it.

"Maybe you're right," he said slowly. He glanced up. "But after what we've been through since your mom died, I thought we could handle anything together."

He sounds so sad! Ashley thought. "We can," she said. "I mean, you're the best dad in the world."

"Yeah," Mary-Kate agreed. "It's just that there are a few things that are easier for us to talk to a woman about. It's a girl thing."

"I understand that," Kevin said. "But I want you to know that no one can love you more than I do."

Mary-Kate hopped out of bed. She sat down on Ashley's bed and put her arms around her father. "We know," she assured him.

"And remember," Kevin added. "There's nothing you can't come to me about."

From the other side, Ashley gave Kevin a big squeeze. "Thanks, Dad!" she said.

Kevin hugged both girls tightly for a moment. Then he stood up and walked towards the door.

"Goodnight, girls," he said.

"Dad?" Ashley called after him. "Could you do us a favour?"

Kevin turned around. "Sure. What is it?"

"Could you . . . knock next time before you come in?" Ashley asked.

"Knock?" Kevin looked surprised. Then he grinned. "Okay. You got it!"

He reached for the doorknob.

"Oh, and Dad?" Mary-Kate called. "One more thing. You don't still think Carrie is too loose, do you?"

A funny look crossed Kevin's face. "I'm not sure any more. Maybe it's me that needs to loosen up," he said.

Mary-Kate and Ashley grinned at each other. All right!

CHAPTER THIRTEEN

"Strike three!" the radio announcer called.

Carrie sat on her rooftop in a lawn chair. Her radio was beside her. She leaned on the safety wall and sighed. "He's not the only one who struck out."

It was the first night after Kevin Burke fired her. Tonight even a Cubs game couldn't cheer her up.

I messed up, she thought. *I should have known he would worry if the girls weren't home. I was wrong.*

But did he have to be so mean? she wondered. *He made me feel like a real worm!*

"That's two outs, and Chicago brings up Sammy Sosa," the announcer said.

"Sammy?" Carrie repeated. She turned up her radio. Sammy Sosa was her favourite Cub. "Come on, Sammy!" she yelled. "Let's see what you're made of!"

She leaned towards the radio and waited for a hit.

"Carrie?" a man's voice called.

Spinning around, Carrie saw Kevin Burke. Her stomach lurched.

"Professor?" she said. She quickly turned the radio down. "Are you making sure that the Cubs are in bed by nine?"

No! she thought as soon as the words were out of her mouth. *My dumb jokes are what got me in trouble before!*

But Kevin just smiled and shook his head.

"The girls told me these were such great seats," he said. "I had to see for myself. I hope you don't mind."

Carrie grinned, feeling more relaxed. "Nah. It's hard to do the wave with just one person," she joked.

Kevin pulled an empty chair over to the table. He pointed to the radio. "So who's up?"

"Sammy Sosa," Carrie said.

"Sammy, huh?" Kevin asked. He turned to the radio and shouted, "Come on, Sammy!

Carrie studied Kevin. He didn't look mad. Just kind of uncomfortable. *What does he have to be uncomfortable about?* she wondered. *I'm the one who got fired!*

"Okay, Professor Burke." She stood up from her chair. "I know you didn't just come up here to cheer Sammy on. What's up?"

"I came here to apologise," Kevin said.

What? Am I hearing him right? Carrie wondered.

She shook her head. "Don't apologise. I kept the girls out too late. And I should have realised you'd be worried. You had every right to fire me."

"I know that," Kevin said. "But— "

Carrie's hurt feelings bubbled up again. "But you didn't have to be so mean about it," she blurted out. "*That* you can apologise for!"

"What?" Kevin exclaimed. He jumped up from his chair and waved his arms. "I was worried to death!"

"And you don't have to yell," Carrie added.

"I never yell!" Kevin yelled.

"You're yelling now!" Carrie yelled back.

"That's because I'm watching a ball game!" Kevin shouted. He leaned over the wall and screamed at the top of his lungs. "Go Cubs! Go Cubs!"

Carrie couldn't hold back a grin.

Kevin turned to face her. "Look, I didn't just come to apologise." He glanced down at his hands. "I-I came here to ask you back."

Carrie stared at him, speechless.

"Excuse me?" she finally said.

"Carrie, I just found out that my little girls aren't little girls any more," Kevin explained. "They're growing up."

Carrie began to see where he was headed. She nodded. "Oh. Spooky, isn't it?" she said sympathetically.

"I'll say," Kevin agreed. "And there are a lot of things they can't talk to me about. Things like— "

"Boys?" Carrie asked.

"Yes!" Kevin said.

"In other words . . . girl stuff," Carrie said.

Kevin nodded. "But they can talk to you."

"Maybe because I've been through a lot of girl stuff myself," Carrie pointed out.

"Well, I haven't," Kevin said. "And that's where you come in. Mary-Kate and Ashley need someone like you in their lives. So I'd like you to come back and work for us."

Carrie's heart was doing major flips. But she was determined to appear cool. Besides, there was something she needed to get straight with Kevin before she said yes.

"Okay. I'll come back," she said. "On one condition."

Kevin sighed. "Carrie, if you expect me to move the lab to eight o'clock— "

"No, no." Carrie laughed. "Nothing like that. Here's the condition: I'm not going to be your spy, Professor Burke."

"Spy?" Kevin asked. "What do you mean?"

"I mean that if Mary-Kate and Ashley tell me something I think you should know, I'll tell you. Otherwise, it's strictly between me and them. Deal?" Carrie held out her hand.

Kevin hesitated a long moment. *Did I blow it?* Carrie wondered.

Then Kevin reached out. Smiling, he shook her hand. "Deal!" he said.

"Good," Carrie said, satisfied. She leaned back in her chair. "Now let's get back to the game."

"Okay," Kevin said. "But before that, I have just one question."

Carrie waved a hand. "Shoot."

"Who's Pokey Valentine?" Kevin asked.

Carrie gave Kevin a sideways look. *Is this a test?* she wondered. Instead of answering, she turned back to the game.

"Come on, Sammy!" she shouted.

"Oh, well," Kevin murmured. "I guess a deal's a deal."

CHAPTER FOURTEEN

"Hi, Brian," Ashley said into the phone. "This is Ashley."

She glanced at the clock. It was just two hours away from the big game. Which meant she had two hours to get out of it!

"I was just calling to see how you were feeling," Ashley went on. "Is, um, is your leg still broken?" she added.

"Only in four places," Brian snapped.

Ashley gulped. "That's really a bummer," she said. "Maybe it would help if you played softball this afternoon. Maybe the exercise would— "

CLICK!

Ashley stared at the phone. *He hung up on me!*

Now what? she wondered. *I've got to get out of this game!*

Suddenly she felt someone grab the phone from her hand. She turned around and saw Mary-Kate grinning at her.

"Nice try," Mary-Kate said.

Ashley gave her sister a pleading look.

"I told you, Mary-Kate," she said. "I'd rather eat worms than play softball."

"Well, you're out of luck," Mary-Kate joked. "We're having hamburgers for dinner tonight."

Mary-Kate and Ashley wore T-shirts with Velcro name tags on the front. On the back was the name of their team: The Belmont Bashers.

"Come on, Ashley," Mary-Kate said. She took an apple from a bowl and polished it on her shirt. "Didn't you learn anything from watching the Cubs game that night on Carrie's rooftop?"

"Sure," Ashley grumbled. "I learned that I want to be a fan, not a player!"

Carrie walked into the kitchen. "I heard that. Fans are important too, you know," she said. She grinned. "And you know I'll be your biggest fan, Ashley. I'll be out there cheering my guts out!"

"Great," Ashley groaned. "While I'm striking my guts out."

The door opened and Jessica and Max walked in.

"Ready, team?" Max asked. He tossed a ball into the air and caught it in his glove.

I'll never be ready, Ashley thought with a sick feeling in her stomach.

"We'd better move," Jessica said. "We saw some kids on their way to the park already."

"Who?" Mary-Kate asked.

"Pokey Valentine and his friends," Jessica said. "They're going to watch the game from the bleachers."

Ashley looked up. Her heart began to pound in her chest. "Did you say . . . Pokey Valentine?" she tried to ask casually.

"Pokey said no way would he miss watching us get creamed," Max said.

Mary-Kate slammed her apple on the counter. "Pokey said that?" she asked angrily.

"Pokey said that?" Ashley echoed with a hollow feeling. She didn't think things could get any worse. But they just did. Pokey Valentine was going to see what a terrible softball player she was!

My life is over, Ashley realised. *This is it!*

At the park, Mary-Kate, Max, and Jessica checked out the opposing team. Ashley checked out the stands for Pokey Valentine.

There he is, she noticed. *Two rows up from Carrie. Middle seat.*

"Were the Dearborn Street kids always that big?" Mary-Kate asked, interrupting her thoughts.

Jessica whistled. "Wow! Look at the size of their pitcher!"

"You mean the huge kid with the braces?" Mary-Kate asked.

"Those aren't braces," Max said with a shiver. "He's chewing on nails."

"Did you check out their studs?" Mary-Kate said. "They look like railroad spikes!"

Ashley clapped her hands over her ears. "Will you please knock it off?" she cried.

A second later she felt a hand on her shoulder. Turning around, she saw Carrie.

"You looked upset, even from way up in the bleachers," Carrie said. She glanced at Max and Jessica. "Guys, can you excuse us a minute? Ashley needs a little pep talk."

"No problem," Jessica said. "Max and I will warm up."

"We're going to need it!" Max said in a hollow voice. He turned and followed Jessica over to the batting cage.

"How are you feeling, kiddo?" Carrie asked Ashley.

"Like I'm about to be humiliated, tortured, and ground to a pulp," Ashley said. "Other than that – fine."

"Come on, Ashley," Mary-Kate urged. "This could be the greatest come-from-behind game ever! I bet you'll hit a home run!"

"I'd rather just run home," Ashley muttered.

Mary-Kate shook her head. "Sometimes I can't believe you're my twin."

Ashley opened her mouth to retort. But she stopped when she saw Carrie's face brighten.

"Hey. That's it!" Carrie cried.

The twins stared at her. "That's what?" Mary-Kate asked.

"The solution to Ashley's problem," Carrie said.

"Huh?" Ashley felt dazed.

Carrie grinned and put an arm around each twin. "Listen up," she said. "Here's the plan… "

CHAPTER FIFTEEN

"Quick. Switch your name tags," Carrie ordered.

"Switch?" Mary-Kate repeated. "What for?"

"This way, you become Ashley and Ashley will become you," Carrie explained.

"Oh, I get it! So when I strike out, everyone will think it's Mary-Kate. Everyone – including Pokey Valentine!" Ashley grinned. "What a great idea!"

Hey! Wait a second! Mary-Kate thought. She scowled. "What a *lousy* idea! I won't do it!"

"Mary-Kate?" Ashley folded her arms. "Remember that ballet recital, back when we were six? And how you were so nervous you couldn't even put on your moth costume?"

Mary-Kate looked down at her sneakers. "Yeah,

I remember," she said slowly.

"Who took your place?" Ashley asked. "Who danced both my butterfly part and your moth part?"

"You did," Mary-Kate admitted.

"And who got the special note from the ballet teacher about what a good recital it was?" Ashley asked, raising an eyebrow.

"I did – I mean, you did," Mary-Kate said.

Ashley spread out her hands. "See? You owe me one, Mary-Kate!"

"She's right," Carrie said, grinning. "You owe her one, girlfriend."

Mary-Kate hesitated. She knew Ashley had a point – but did she really have to humiliate herself this way?

"Come on." Carrie gave Mary-Kate's hair a gentle tug. "She's your sister. And this is really important to her. This is what families do for each other."

"Okay." Sighing, Mary-Kate tugged at her name tag. "Let the switcheroo begin."

"Now you're talking!" Ashley said.

The twins quickly switched name tags. Now Mary-Kate was Ashley and Ashley was Mary-Kate.

"Very convincing," Carrie said. "I just hope you guys can keep it up."

"Me too," Mary-Kate said. "We might fool the kids from Dearborn Street. But can we fool our friends? I mean, Ashley is a little taller than me."

Just then Jessica ran up. "Come on, Mary-Kate," she called. "The game's starting – and you're up first."

And she grabbed Ashley's arm!

As Jessica pulled her away, Ashley glanced over her shoulder and grinned at Mary-Kate.

"Wow," Mary-Kate murmured. "I guess we *can* fool our friends!"

"Makes me wish I had a twin," Carrie said. She patted Mary-Kate on the shoulder. "You did a nice thing, kiddo. You're a good sister. Now go play your best!"

The Dearborn Devils took their positions on the field. Mary-Kate sat on the bench between Max and Jessica. She could see Ashley taking the bat in shaky hands.

"I'm glad Mary-Kate is up first," Jessica said. "She's the best player we have."

Mary-Kate puffed out her chest. "Thanks!" she almost said. But just in time, she remembered: She was supposed to be Ashley!

"Uh, right. She's okay, I guess," she said instead. She watched Ashley step up to the plate. *I hate this*, she thought. *I wish that really was me up there!*

"Come on, Mary-Kate!" Max screamed from the bench.

Mary-Kate stared at her twin. Ashley looked so nervous!

I've got to help her, Mary-Kate realised. *She needs me!*

"Go, Mary-Kate!" Mary-Kate yelled. "Knock 'em dead!"

At the plate, Ashley glanced around. She gave her sister the thumbs-up.

Just as the pitcher wound up for his first throw!

"No! Keep your eye on the ball!" Mary-Kate yelled.

"Ball?" Ashley looked puzzled. "What ball?"

"*That* ball!" Mary-Kate screamed. She pointed at the softball that was whizzing towards home plate.

"Help!" Ashley cried. She squeezed her eyes shut.

"Steee-riiiiike!" the umpire shouted.

Jessica jumped up from the bench. "A strike? That's not like Mary-Kate!"

Mary-Kate slumped over and buried her head in her hands. *Ashley's my sister and I want to be there for her*, she thought. *But does it have to be this hard? My reputation is going to be ruined!*

Mary-Kate watched nervously as Ashley got a second strike. At least she swung the bat that time, Mary-Kate thought.

The pitcher sent another ball whizzing towards the plate. Ashley choked up her grip on the bat. She swung.

CRACK!

It was a hit!

"All right!" Carrie screamed from the bleachers.

"Run!" Mary-Kate shouted. "Run to first!"

Ashley threw down the bat and ran towards first base.

Mary-Kate watched tensely as the ball bounced into the outfield. One of the fielders scooped it up and threw it to the first baseman, a tall, red-haired girl.

"Got you!" the girl yelled, and tagged Ashley with the ball.

"You're out!" the umpire bellowed.

Ashley trudged back towards the bench. Mary-Kate gave her a sympathetic pat on the shoulder. "Nice try, Ash— uh, Mary-Kate," Mary-Kate said.

"Yeah. I almost made it, didn't I?" Ashley said.

The twins grinned at each other. And suddenly Mary-Kate felt better.

Even if we don't win the game, at least Ashley will have a good time today, she thought. *And so what about my reputation? I'll just tell everyone I had an off day. Even major leaguers have off days sometimes. Right?*

She tugged her baseball cap down on her forehead.

"Let's play ball!" she hollered.

At the bottom of the ninth inning, the score was tied, the Bashers were up – and the bases were full!

Max looked at the line-up sheet and shuddered.

"You look like you're going to hurl, Max," Ashley commented. "What's wrong?"

"Your sister Ashley is up next," Max said glumly.

Ashley shot a glance at Mary-Kate.

Mary-Kate folded her arms. "Don't count me out until you've seen me play, Max," she snapped. Then she grabbed a bat and walked into the cage.

Ashley watched Mary-Kate warm up with the bat. She could hear her team mates muttering.

"Oh, great," Natasha Sims said. "The bases are full – and get a load of who's up. Ashley Burke!"

Quincy Parker shook his head. "That's it. We're dead meat."

Ashley bit her lip. *Am I really that bad?* she wondered.

Suddenly she saw Carrie stand up and hurry over from the stands.

"Hey, you guys!" Carrie shouted to the team.

"I've seen more team spirit at a doughnut factory. Let's cheer Ashley on!"

The Bashers stared at Carrie as she began to chant:

"Ash-ley! Ash-ley! Ash-ley!"

The Bashers shrugged. Then they began to chant, too.

"Ash-ley! Ash-ley! Ash-ley!"

Carrie faced the stands and motioned for them to join in.

"Ash-ley! Ash-ley! Ash-ley!"

Ashley looked around. Everyone was cheering her name – even Pokey Valentine!

Wow, Ashley thought. *I know they're really cheering for Mary-Kate, but who cares? It feels great!*

The field grew quiet as Mary-Kate gripped the bat. Ashley could see her glaring at the pitcher. She's trying to psych him out, Ashley guessed.

The pitcher nodded to the catcher. Then he reached back and threw the ball.

"Whoa!" Max muttered. "A knuckleball!"

Ashley tensed. She recalled Mary-Kate asking Carrie about knuckleballs. Would Mary-Kate remember what Carrie taught her?

Mary-Kate swung the bat.

CRACK! It connected solidly with the ball.

The ball soared over the pitcher's head – and right into the stands!

"Run!" Carrie shouted. "Run home!"

"Run!" Ashley echoed.

Everyone was on their feet as Mary-Kate ran to first base, then to second, then to third. The crowd went wild as the other team members ran to home, one by one.

"It's a grand slam!" Jessica cried.

"Ashley saved the day!" Max cheered.

No, Ashley thought. *Carrie and Mary-Kate did . . . but I get all the credit!*

I think I'm starting to like this game!

CHAPTER SIXTEEN

"Hey, guys," Kevin said. As the twins and Carrie walked into the living room, he glanced up from the papers he was grading. "Who won the game?"

"We did," Mary-Kate said. "And Ashley got the winning hit."

"Yeah," Ashley said. "I hit a rope up the middle!"

Kevin looked at the girls suspiciously. "A rope?"

"It's hitting it well enough to get to first base," Carrie explained.

"*I* know what it is," Kevin said. "But Ashley doesn't."

The twins looked at each other and laughed.

"Busted!" they said together. Then they pulled off their name tags and exchanged them.

Kevin's eyes narrowed. "Hey! Did you girls play some kind of twin trick?"

"Look, Dad," Ashley said. "I know that in the movies the crummiest hitter always comes through, but I *really* stink. And this way, I got to be a hero!"

Kevin stood up from the sofa. "But you're not really the hero. Mary-Kate got the hit."

"Okay, okay, I have a confession," Carrie said, raising her hand. "The whole thing was my idea."

Kevin frowned. "Carrie, the twins shouldn't be encouraged to play tricks like that. It's sneaky! It's dishonest! It's— "

"Come on, Professor," Carrie broke in. "Who got hurt? And Ashley had a great day. You have to admit, it was a good idea."

Kevin shut his mouth tightly. The twins stared nervously at him.

"Do you think he's going to fire Carrie again?" Ashley whispered to Mary-Kate. Carrie had told them about how she got fired and rehired in her first week.

Then a slow smile spread across Kevin's face.

"I guess it was pretty clever, at that." Kevin chuckled. "Let's not make a habit of it, but – thanks, Carrie."

"Don't mention it, Professor Burke," Carrie said.

89

Mary-Kate and Ashley exchanged relieved glances. Carrie wasn't going anywhere.

"Hey, is that my paper you're grading?" Carrie asked. She bent over the stack of papers in Kevin's hand. She pointed to one of Kevin's notes. "Can we discuss this? Here's what I was thinking . . . "

She looks so at home, Ashley thought, watching them.

Mary-Kate was obviously thinking the same thing. "She's like part of the family," she whispered, grinning at Ashley.

Ashley returned the grin. Yeah. Carrie *was* practically part of the family already. It was amazing how well she fitted in. It was almost as if they'd all been waiting for her to come along.

Now she was here – and that made them a real winning team!

Mary-Kate & Ashley's Scrapbook

Breakfast on the
first day of school...

we were so
excited!

Two of a Kind

Until Dad
told us . . .

that we needed
a babysitter!

We had to
put our
heads
together to
make a plan!

"Let's sleep on it," Ashley said.

"Let's ask Max," said Mary-Kate.

Then we found Carrie!

All we had to do was convince Dad that she
was the one!

"Dad ! We found the perfect babysitter!"

We can always
convince Dad.

How? It's a
Twin Thing!

PSSST! Take a sneak peak
at

How to Flunk Your First Date

Mary-Kate trudged up the stairs to her room. Her head was spinning with numbers. Fractions. Decimals. Percents.

How come Ashley got all the brains in the maths department? she wondered. It didn't seem fair!

Ashley was lying on her bed, flipping through a magazine. She leaped up when Mary-Kate walked in.

"Did Taylor leave already?" she demanded. "I wanted to say goodbye."

Mary-Kate rolled her eyes. Taylor was her new maths tutor – and Ashley had a major crush on him!

"He's gone. But he'll be back tomorrow," Mary-Kate reported glumly.

"Did he say anything about me?" Ashley asked eagerly.

"Yeah. He said with all the sodas you came down

to get, you must have a bladder the size of Lake Michigan!" Mary-Kate answered.

Ashley beamed. "So he did notice me," she cooed.

Mary-Kate flopped down on her own bed. She wasn't in the mood to talk about boys right now.

She was too worried about missing her after-school basketball practice. It was the same time as her tutoring sessions. If she missed too many practices, Coach wouldn't let her play in the big game!

Ashley hurried over and sat down beside her.

"Listen," she said, "what if I told you I might have a way to get you out of tutoring – and back on the basketball court?"

Mary-Kate sat up fast. "Are you kidding? How?"

Ashley lowered her voice. "We could switch places – and I could go to your tutoring sessions," she suggested.

Mary-Kate stared at Ashley. "You mean you'd really do that?" she asked, amazed.

"Of course. You're my twin sister," Ashley said. "I couldn't stand for you to miss the big basketball game!"

"Yeah, right," Mary-Kate cracked. "Don't lie – you've got a thing for Taylor, haven't you?"

"He is so gorgeous!" Ashley burst out. She nudged Mary-Kate with her shoulder. "So should we switch? What do you say?"

mary-kateandashley

TWO of a kind ™

Coming soon – can you collect them all?

HarperCollins*Entertainment*

mary-kateandashley

Meet Chloe and Riley Carlson.

So much to do...

so little time

(1)	How to Train a Boy	(0 00 714458 X)
(2)	Instant Boyfriend	(0 00 714448 2)
(3)	Too Good to be True	(0 00 714449 0)
(4)	Just Between Us	(0 00 714450 4)
(5)	Tell Me About It	(0 00 714451 2)
(6)	Secret Crush	(0 00 714452 0)

*... and more
to come!*

HarperCollins*Entertainment*

PARACHUTE PRESS

DUALSTAR PUBLICATIONS

mary-kateandashley.com
AOL Keyword: mary-kateandashley

Mary-Kate and Ashley in their latest movie adventure

Available on video from 11th March

Get ready to celebrate with the Real Dolls for Real Girls

Mary-Kate & Ashley Birthday Bash Fashion Dolls!

Celebrate with birthday cake, present, and a camera to capture the memories!

Plus a hip floral halter dress included for trendy birthday style!

DUALSTAR CONSUMER PRODUCTS

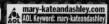

Order Form

To order direct from the publishers, just make a list of the titles you want and fill in the form below:

Name ....

Address ....

....

....

Send to: Dept 6, HarperCollins Publishers Ltd, Westerhill Road, Bishopbriggs, Glasgow G64 2QT.

Please enclose a cheque or postal order to the value of the cover price, plus:

UK & BFPO: Add £1.00 for the first book, and 25p per copy for each additional book ordered.

Overseas and Eire: Add £2.95 service charge. Books will be sent by surface mail but quotes for airmail despatch will be given on request.

A 24-hour telephone ordering service is available to holders of Visa, MasterCard, Amex or Switch cards on 0141- 772 2281.

Collins
An *Imprint* of HarperCollins*Publishers*